Bunny's EASTER EGG

Written and illustrated by
Anne Mortimer

KATHERINE TEGEN BOOKS
An Imprint of HarperCollins *Publishers*

Bunny's Easter Egg
Copyright © 2010 by Anne Mortimer
Manufactured in China.

Library of Congress Cataloging-in-Publication Data
Mortimer, Anne.
Bunny's Easter egg / written and illustrated by Anne Mortimer. — 1st ed.
p. cm.
Summary: Bunny is exhausted after spending the night hiding eggs for the Easter egg hunt,
but she cannot find a comfortable, quiet place to sleep.
ISBN 978-0-06-136664-2 (trade bdg.) — ISBN 978-0-06-136665-9 (lib. bdg.)
[1. Rabbits—Fiction.   2. Sleep—Fiction.   3. Eggs—Fiction.   4. Easter—Fiction.]   I. Title.
PZ7.M8465Bun   2010   2008031237   [E]—dc22   CIP   AC

Typography by Rachel Zegar
10   11   12   13   14   SCP   10   9   8   7   6   5   4   3   2   1
❖
First Edition

For my mother
and a very special thank-you
to Katherine for inspiring me

—A.M.

There are thirteen colored eggs hidden in the pictures.
Can you find them all?

It was early Easter morning.
Bunny was very tired.
All night she had been hiding eggs
for the Easter egg hunt.

There was just one very plain egg left to hide.
Bunny was far too tired to hide the last egg,
so, with a hop, a skip, and a jump,
she brought the egg into her basket
and closed her eyes.

Suddenly she heard a crackling sound.
Something moved and bumped,
and Bunny leaped out of the basket.

"Oh no!" cried Bunny.
"I can't sleep here. It's far too busy."

With a hop, a skip, and a jump,
Bunny landed in the hollow of an old oak tree.
She curled her ears, twitched her nose,
and closed her eyes.

Some young birds sang very loudly.
Cheep, cheep, chirrup, chirrup, went the birds.

"Oh no!" cried Bunny.
"I can't sleep here. It's far too noisy."

Bunny leaped out of the hollow
and with a hop, a skip, and a jump
headed for the garden shed.

She jumped into the wheelbarrow
and curled her ears, twitched her nose,
and closed her eyes.

A hedgehog woke her up.
Prickle, prickle, prickle, went the hedgehog.

"Oh no!" cried Bunny.
"I can't sleep here. It's far too painful."

With a hop, a skip, and a jump,
Bunny found herself in the garden.

There she discovered an old pot.
Bunny crawled in, burrowing down to sleep.
She curled her ears, twitched her nose,
and closed her eyes.

Some mice woke her up.
Squeak, squeak, squeak, went the mice.

"Oh no!" cried Bunny.
"I can't sleep here. It's far too squeaky."

With a hop, a skip, and a jump,
she ran to the flower garden
and burrowed into a warm, soft patch of grass.
She curled her ears, twitched her nose,
and closed her eyes.

A mole woke her up.
Push, *push*, *prod*, went the mole.

"Oh no!" cried Bunny.
"I can't sleep here. It's far too lumpy."

With a hop, a skip, and a jump,
she leaped into a boat on the lily pond.
She curled her ears, twitched her nose,
and closed her eyes.

Two ducks and a frog woke her up.
Quack, quack, quack, went the ducks.
Croak, croak, croak, went the frog.

"Oh no!" cried Bunny.
"I can't sleep here. It's far too wet!"

With a hop, a skip, and a jump,

Bunny went into the greenhouse.

There she found a deep seed tray to burrow into.

She curled her ears, twitched her nose,

and closed her eyes.

Two kittens pounced on top of her.

Meow, purr, meow, went the kittens.

"Oh no!" cried Bunny.

"I can't sleep here. They won't leave me alone!"

She headed back to where she had begun.

Wearily, Bunny found her favorite basket.
The plain egg was nowhere to be seen.

Bunny burrowed down among the sweet-scented flowers.
She curled her ears, twitched her nose,
and closed her eyes.

"*Mmmmmm,*" she murmured.
At last, this is perfect, thought Bunny.

Bunny didn't sleep for long.
The plain egg had hatched,
and Bunny had a new friend
who wasn't noisy, prickly, lumpy, or pesky.

HAPPY EASTER, BUNNY!